For Maddison Jane Piatt,
in case she falls off a turnip truck
—J.Y.

To beautiful little Hanah
—V.V.

The Flying Witch
Text copyright © 2003 by Jane Yolen
Illustrations copyright © 2003 by Vladimir Vagin
Manufactured in China. All rights reserved.
www.harperchildrens.com

Library of Congress Cataloging-in-Publication Data
Yolen, Jane.
The flying witch / by Jane Yolen ; illustrated by Vladimir Vagin.
p.   cm.
Summary: Relates how a turnip farmer's daughter outwits the fearsome witch Baba Yaga.
ISBN 0-06-028536-2 — ISBN 0-06-028537-0 (lib. bdg.)
1. Baba Yaga (Legendary character)—Legends.   [1. Baba Yaga (Legendary character)
—Legends.
2. Fairy tales.   3. Folklore—Russia.}   I. Vagin, Vladimir Vasil'evich, 1937– ill.   II. Title.
PZ8.Y78 Fl   2002
398.2'0947'01—dc21   00-057265
[E]

Typography by Al Cetta
1 2 3 4 5 6 7 8 9 10
❖
First Edition

The Flying Witch

by Jane Yolen · illustrated by Vladimir Vagin

HARPERCOLLINSPUBLISHERS

*W*hirrr. *Whirr. Clunkety-clank.*
Something flew over the dark tangled forest.

It was Baba Yaga, the Russian witch, in her mortar and pestle.

The mortar looked like a large wooden drinking cup, the pestle like a club. They were both very old and very rickety. They made a great racket. A rickety-racket.

When Baba Yaga wanted to go up, she pulled on the pestle.

When Baba Yaga wanted to go down, she pushed on the pestle.

Sometimes she even flew upside down.
Whirrr. Whirr. Clunkety-clank.

Baba Yaga skimmed over the treetops
looking for plump young children to
eat. But plump young children were
difficult to find in a dark tangled forest.
So every day she went home to a
supper of cold, thin soup.

"Pfooie!" said Baba Yaga, and sniffed
with her long iron nose. "Not even a turnip
in it!" How she wished for something more in
her soup.

Now one day a small girl—not really plump and not really skinny but somewhere in between—wandered into the forest.

She had fallen off the back of her father's turnip truck as he sped through the winding paths on his way to market. *Clangety-clang.*

The girl dusted herself off and watched the truck speed away.

"Well," she said aloud, "I have two good feet and a fine sense of direction. I will go through the forest on my own."

She walked and walked for a very long time until she was quite tired.

Just then who should cruise overhead but . . .

Whirrr. Whirr. Clunkety-clank.

Baba Yaga saw the girl and grinned. "Not really plump. But not really skinny either." She pushed on the pestle, and the mortar flew down to the forest floor.

"Little girl, little girl, where are you going?" asked Baba Yaga.

Now the little girl knew better than to talk to strangers. And who could have been stranger than Baba Yaga, with her greasy hair and her long iron nose? Besides, her father had often warned her about witches. "Witches," he said, "eat little girls."

But the little girl had been walking for a long time, and she was very, very tired.

"I am following my father's truck to the market," she said.

"Well, climb in," Baba Yaga told her. "I am going there myself."

So into the mortar climbed the little girl, but she was careful to stay as far from the witch as possible.

Off they flew into the sky.

Whirrr. Whirr. Clunkety-clank.

But did they go to the market? Oh, no! They flew straight to
Baba Yaga's house, which was way in the middle of the forest.

"Something is not right," thought the little girl. "But I have two good feet, a fine sense of direction, two strong arms, and a clever mind. I will get away on my own."

Baba Yaga pushed on the pestle, and the mortar flew down, landing in back of a strange little house.

The house squatted on two scaly chicken feet.

Getting out of the mortar, Baba Yaga called:

*"Turn, little hut, turn.
Stand with your back to the old oak tree.
Stand with your front door open to me."*

The house creaked and turned around.

Grabbing the little girl by the arm, Baba Yaga pulled her in.

Baba Yaga locked the door and put a great pot on the fire. "I am tired of thin soup. I am ready for a plump young girl."

The girl thought quickly, then held out her arm. "I am not nearly plump enough to eat," she said. "But if you fatten me for a few days, I will be ready."

Baba Yaga looked at the child's arm. Really, the child was right. She was not plump at all. But what could she fatten the child with? Surely not thin soup!

"My father's truck is full of turnips," said the child. "They can make me fat. If you fly to the market and buy up all his turnips, I will cook them for you. I cook for my father all the time. When I am fat enough, you can eat me."

"What a good idea," said Baba Yaga. She locked the little girl in the house with magic.

Then off Baba Yaga flew in her mortar and pestle.

Whirrr. Whirr. Clunkety-clank.

She flew straight to the market, where the farmer had just arrived.

Baba Yaga said, "Farmer, I hear you have great turnips. I want them all." And she held out a bag full of coins.

But of course, when the farmer unloaded the truck, he saw his daughter was missing.

Then he noticed Baba Yaga's greasy hair and her long iron nose. He wondered who had told her about his great turnips. He put two and two and two together and guessed what had happened. But he did not say a word.

Baba Yaga left, flying off in her mortar. *Whirrr. Whirr.*
Clunkety-clank.

She flew, but not very high. Her mortar was heavy with
all those turnips.

The farmer easily followed her in his truck.
Clangety-clang.

As soon as the old witch landed in the
middle of the forest, the farmer got out of his
truck and crept through the trees.

He heard her call to the house:

"Turn, little hut, turn.
Stand with your back to the old oak tree.
Stand with your front door open to me."

Then she opened the door and went in.

"Little girl, little girl, I am home," said Baba Yaga.

The little girl saw the turnips and smiled. She knew her father would guess where she was. But still, he might not come in time.

"You sit right there in your comfortable chair," said the little girl. "And I will make us a great big bowl of turnip stew."

Baba Yaga sat in the chair and set her bony feet up on a cushion. No one had ever offered to make her dinner before. Yes—she liked this feisty little girl.

So the little girl put more wood in the stove, and the pot of water began to boil. She washed the turnips and cut them into small bits.

Plip-plop. Plip-plop. She dropped the bits into the pot.

A bit of salt. A bit of pepper. A bit of green herbs.

Plip-plop. Plip-plop.

Soon the turnips were boiling merrily.

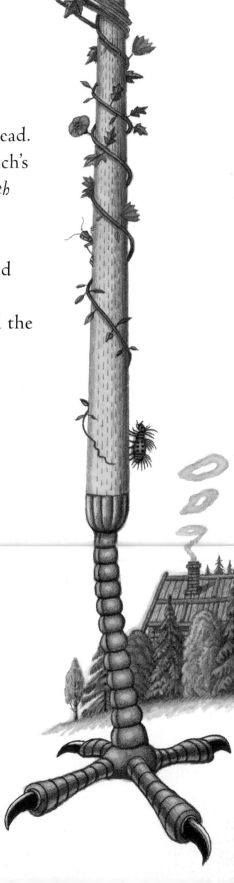

Meanwhile, outside the hut, the farmer wondered what he should do.

He paced and paced and scratched his head. He knew that one should not go into a witch's house without a proper invitation. Even *with* an invitation it was dangerous.

But when smoke began to curl from the chimney—*swish-swish-swish*—he felt he could wait no longer.

He went up to the little house and used the same words Baba Yaga had.

"Turn, little hut, turn.
Stand with your back to the old oak tree.
Stand with your front door open to me."

The little house turned, and the farmer raced through the open front door.

What do you think he saw?

His little daughter was feeding turnip stew to the old witch.

"One for you," said the little girl. "And one for me."

Baba Yaga's eyes were closed. Her long iron nose shone. She was smiling. "Yummm," she said. "Better than plump children. Hot and filling."

"And much less trouble," said the little girl with a smile.

So the farmer and his daughter stayed for dinner. And they promised to bring back more turnips the next week.

Or perhaps potatoes.

Then they got into the truck and drove home.
Clangety-clang.
Clangety-clang.
Clangety-clang.

ABOUT BABA YAGA

There are dozens of Baba Yaga stories in Russia and its neighboring countries.

Baba Yaga is always a female fiend who devours humans, though sometimes she is kind to feisty children. She is usually portrayed as a tall, gaunt hag with disheveled hair. In some of the Russian tales she is first met lying stretched out in her hut: her head in the front, her right leg in one corner, her left leg in the other, and her long iron nose through the roof.

When her hut is properly addressed, it turns around. (I have made up a rhyme but used words from the old Russian tales: "Turn about little hut, put your back to the forest, your front to me.") In the old stories there is always a fence of human bones around the hut.

Baba Yaga is distinguished from other witches in folklore by her chicken-footed hut and by her mortar and pestle. In some of the stories she brushes away the traces of her flight with a broom.

I found a number of Baba Yaga stories in W. R. S. Ralston's *Russian Folk-Tales* (New York: Arno Press, 1977), the classic Aleksandr Afanas'ev's *Russian Fairy Tales* (New York: Pantheon Books, 1945, 1973), and *The Three Kingdoms: Russian Folk Tales from Aleksandr Afanas'ev's Collection* (Moscow: Raduga Publishers, 1985.) But this one is really my own.